Title: King Flashypants and the Toys of Terror
On Sale: 11/13/2018
Price: $13.99
Ages: 7-10

KING FLASHYPANTS

AND THE Toys of Terror

KING FLASHYPANTS

AND THE
Toys of Terror

BOOK 3

WRITTEN AND DRAWN BY **ANDY RILEY**

Henry Holt and Company · New York

Henry Holt and Company, *Publishers since 1866*
Henry Holt® is a registered trademark of Macmillan Publishing Group, LLC
175 Fifth Avenue, New York, NY 10010 • mackids.com

ISBN 978-1-62779-813-6
Library of Congress Control Number 2018936449

Our books may be purchased in bulk for promotional, educational, or business
use. Please contact your local bookseller or the Macmillan Corporate and
Premium Sales Department at (800) 221-7945 ext. 5442 or by e-mail at
MacmillanSpecialMarkets@macmillan.com.

Originally published in 2017 in Great Britain by Hodder and Stoughton
First American edition, 2018 / Design by Jennifer Stephenson
Printed in the United States of America by LSC Communications,
Harrisonburg, Virginia

1   3   5   7   9   10   8   6   4   2

With thanks to
Polly Faber, Bill Riley, Eddie Riley,
Emma Goldhawk, Jennifer Stephenson,
Anne McNeil, Gordon Wise,
Hilary Murray Hill, Lucy Upton,
Stephanie Allen, Jennifer Breslin,
Emily Thomas, Kevin Cecil,
Greta Riley, and Robin Riley

Dedicated to Daisy Wilson

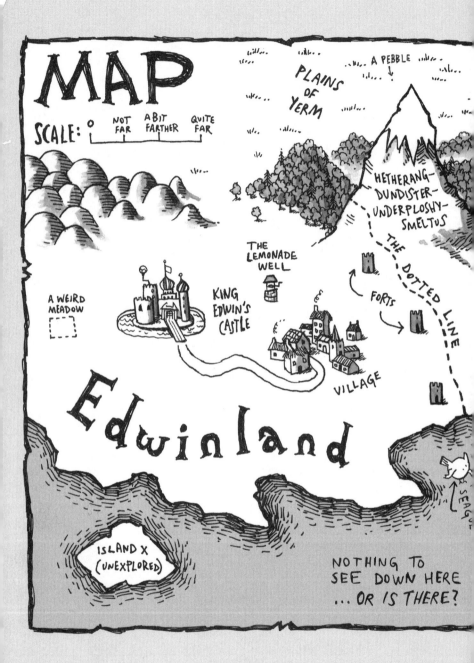

KING EDWIN
FLASHYPANTS

MINISTER
JILL

MEGAN
THE JESTER

EMPEROR NURBISON

THE OLD EMPRESS VERONICA

GLOBULUS

Just imagine how exciting all these chapters must be

The Ninth of Janvember

Long, long ago, there was a time called "the olden days." The olden days came before nowadays, which is when we live. But it came *after* "the olden olden days," when everybody lived in caves and spoke in grunts and hit each other with clubs all day.

OLDEN OLDEN DAYS   OLDEN DAYS   NOWADAYS

The olden days was a time of magic and monsters and knights and castles. And in one of those castles there lived a nine-year-old boy. His name was King Edwin Flashypants, and he was about to hide inside a box of cornflakes.

If you try this in your kitchen, you won't fit, unless you've just shrunk to the size of a pencil case—and if you have, then please see a doctor right away. But Edwin was a king, so he had a giant box

of cereal specially made for banquets. It was as big as a mattress.

His friends gave him a leg up. He tumbled inside with a **FLUMP-SCRUNCH** and poked two holes in the cardboard so he could see out.

"She'll be waking up soon!" said Edwin. "Everybody hide, quick as you can!"

Edwin's pals hurried around the castle's kitchen.

Minister Jill, the grown-up who helped Edwin with the difficult bits of running a kingdom, crawled into a sack of potatoes.

Centurion Alisha and her palace
guards hid among the pots and pans.

Baxter the Hermit, whose beard was longer than he was, did a headstand in a vase. He was pretending to be a potted plant.

"Baxter, she'll see you there for sure," said King Edwin, but Baxter couldn't hear because his ears were full of dirt.

Upstairs in the castle, an alarm clock went **BONG**.

Megan the Jester jumped out of her jester-shaped bed. She checked the calendar.

"The ninth of Janvember!" said Megan. *"It's my birthday!"*

She was so excited, she slid down
all the banisters in the castle, knocking
over Minister Jill's signs that said *Please
Don't Slide Down the Banisters*.
Then she ran to the kitchen, where she
knew that Edwin and all her friends would
be waiting to give her a special birthday
breakfast.

But the kitchen
was quiet.

"Nobody here,"
said Megan.

"Everything's
normal, except for
that weird hairy
plant on the
table."

She slumped down on the potato
sack. For a second, she thought she heard a
potato say, "Ouch."

"I suppose I'll have to make my *own*
birthday breakfast," sighed Megan.

She hefted the giant box of cornflakes
off the counter. It seemed heavier than
normal. Then she tipped it over her favorite
bowl. Out came a thousand cornflakes—
and a nine-year-old king.

"Surprise!"
shouted
Edwin.

"SURPRISE!" shouted everybody else as they jumped out from their hiding places.

"You did remember, you did, you did!" said Megan. She couldn't have been happier.

"And now for the birthday presents!" said Edwin.

Centurion Alisha and the other palace guards gave Megan a pogo stick.

"It's a pogo stick," said Centurion Alisha.

"Thanks—oOf!

Just what I—oOf!—

wanted—oOf!"

said Megan, who

was already pogoing her head into the kitchen ceiling.

"I wasn't sure what you'd like, so I

thought I'd give you money," said Minister Jill. There are some grown-ups who always do that, and Jill was one of them.

Baxter gave Megan a single glove and promised that if she wore it a lot, he would buy her a matching one next year.

"I've *made* you a present," said King Edwin. "Just close your eyes, Megan . . ."

Megan closed her eyes. She hoped it

was going to be as wonderful as a pogo
stick, money, or a single glove.

"Open them!" said Edwin.

Megan looked. There was a mirror
in front of her—and in the mirror, Megan
saw she was wearing a hat made from a
cardboard box. Paper lightning
bolts were held on
with tape.

There was a cape made from a comforter around her shoulders. Edwin looked just as strange. What was this all about?

"Hope you like my present, Megan. It's an idea I've had. We're going to play

SUPERHEROES!"

Because this was the olden days, and Edwin was the first person ever to think of superheroes, he had to explain what they were.

"Superheroes have costumes and exciting names, and they go around fighting baddies and saving the world with their superpowers!"

"Are superpowers like magic powers?" said Megan.

"No," said Edwin. "Superpowers are different. They're *super.*"

Nobody quite understood the difference, but because Edwin was the king, everyone nodded as if they did.

Edwin handed Megan some Hero Information Cards with everything she needed to know.

HERO NAME: THUNDERCLOUD

ORIGIN: BITTEN BY A MUTANT CLOUD WITH TEETH MADE OF RAIN

SUPER POWERS: DRIZZLE, POGO STICK MEGA-BOUNCE

THUNDERCLOUD IS A MEMBER OF THE SUPERHERO TEAM "WARRIORS OF AMAZING JUSTICE"

HERO NAME: SHARK BOY

ORIGIN: ONE DAY, JUST DECIDED SHARKS WERE AWESOME

SUPER POWERS: JUDO, SHARK TICKLE

SHARK BOY IS A MEMBER OF THE SUPERHERO TEAM "WARRIORS OF AMAZING JUSTICE"

Minister Jill thought, *Clouds don't have teeth. And sharks can't tickle. This is nonsense. No, I think Megan would have liked a better present, like a nice vase or some light-brown socks or . . .*

"I love it!" said Megan. "Hey, Shark Boy, let's play superheroes!"

First, they all ate a really special birthday breakfast, with

treats like eggs made out of sausage,
and sausages made out of egg. Then
King Edwin and Megan the Jester played
superheroes for the rest of the
morning. They saved
the world from alien
invaders and
mechanical
monsters.

Think of the best playtime you've ever had with your favorite friend. Now picture that day, but in a big castle full of slides and tunnels and trapdoors. That was the day Edwin and Megan had.

"Imagine if Warriors of Amazing Justice had to fight *real* villains," said Edwin.

"But the only baddie around here

is Emperor Nurbison, and I don't think he'll try anything again," said Megan.

"Ha-ha! Not since we beat him twice, no!"

"We're totally safe forever," said Megan.

For a second, Edwin wondered if being a bit more worried about Emperor Nurbison would be a good thing for a king to do.

Then he thought, *Let's go and eat chips.*

The Cottage and the Cupboard

Emperor Nurbison was all about the hating. Hating was his hobby. He loved to hate stuff, and he hated to love stuff.

He hated white cats because they ran away whenever he tried to stroke them, even though villains are *supposed*

to stroke white cats. He hated rainbows
because their pretty colors cheered
everybody up. He hadn't yet found a
way to chop rainbows down when they
appeared, even though he had tried lots
of times with a big ax. He hated King
Edwin Flashypants most of all, because
Edwin stopped him from invading the
annoyingly happy and un-hatey place
called Edwinland.

The list of things Emperor Nurbison actually *liked* was very short. There wasn't much on it except "being evil" and "pointy boots."

But even the evilest emperors have to go to visit their mom sometimes.

Nurbison's mom was named Veronica, and she was once an evil empress feared all over the world. Then her knees went. So she retired to a little cottage by the sea with roses climbing all around the front door. Veronica being as evil as she was, they were man-eating roses.

"Globulus! To my side!" said the emperor, and his loyal assistant scurried forward.

"I don't want those roses nipping at my handsome beard when I go in," said the emperor. "But they won't bother me if they're busy chomping your face off, will they, Globulus?"

"You know, like, well, the thing is," said Globulus, "them roses are proper scary, kind of thing, so I—"

The emperor rolled Globulus at the roses.

Globulus was the size and shape of a
bowling ball, so this wasn't too hard.

Globulus bumped into the biggest flower.
It didn't even twitch.

"Good!" said the emperor. "They must
be asleep."

Nurbison strode straight for the door. Five
roses gnashed him with their thorny jaws.

After leaving Globulus to fight the roses—and after realizing he could have gone in through the back door—the emperor was in the cottage, having tea with his mother.

"Can I tempt you with a cookie, my darling Nurbly-Nibs?" said Empress Veronica, holding out a tray.

"DEAD STARFISH" COOKIE, MADE FROM A DEAD STARFISH

TRIPLE-DECKER CHOCOLATE COOKIE WITH WHITE CHOCOLATE CHIPS

RANCID NINE-YEAR-OLD WAFER

DRIED POND SLIME COOKIE WITH A ROTTEN CHERRY ON TOP

SNOTTERDOODLE

Nurbison took the chocolate cookie with white chocolate chips. When he bit into it, he discovered the white chocolate chips were really maggots. If you've ever seen dogs wriggle through a line of poles at a dog show— that's what the little creatures were doing around the emperor's teeth.

"Thank you, Mother," Nurbison muttered.

"Ha! Ha! Ha! The old maggoty cookie prank! Not very dastardly, I know, but it's the best I can do at my age," said Veronica. "So, son, you're an evil emperor—what kind of evilness have you been up to?"

"What evilness *haven't* I been up to, more like! **FOO HOO HOO HOO**, Mother, **FOO HOO HOO HOO!**"

"Foo hoo hoo hoo" was Emperor Nurbison's evil laugh. It could even scare things that don't normally get scared, like tigers or loaves of bread. But no matter how hard he tried—and he *was* trying—he wasn't sure it was working on his mom.

"Ah, the horrors I have unleashed upon this world!" said Emperor Nurbison. "I poured salt into a sugar bowl, ruining several mugs of tea! I made a pigeon cry by calling it Stumpy Toes! I glued a penny to the pavement, then watched people try to pick it up! Truly, my wickedness knows no bounds! And then I—"

"PAH!" said Veronica. "That's not evil, that's just a bit naughty. A *truly* evil emperor wouldn't get beaten—twice!—by Edwin Flashypants. You can't even seize a kingdom from a little boy!"

The emperor looked at his shoes. Mom had a point.

"Back in the day, son," said Veronica,

"I would have mashed him to paste. Then
fed the paste to the wolves. Then blown
up the wolves."

She struggled out of her chair, rummaged in a dark cupboard, and pulled out a picture in a grimy old frame. She blew the dust off, making sure to get most of it in Emperor Nurbison's face.

"Quite something when I was young, wasn't I?" she said. "Sword as long as a giraffe's trousers. Eye patch, even though both my eyes were perfectly fine. Kept bumping into things, but oh, I looked terrifying! The things I got up to . . ."

Emperor Nurbison had heard this speech before. But he wasn't looking at the picture. He was staring at something that had tumbled out of the cupboard as the empress had been rummaging. Something he hadn't seen since he was a small child.

A doll.

Years ago, when Nurbison was a boy, his mother had kept it on a shelf. It had beautiful black shiny hair and big gleaming eyes. He used to find it a bit scary.

". . . so I boiled the king of the Ant-People with hot water from a massive kettle, and then . . . Nurbison, why are you staring at that useless old magic doll?"

"It's magic? Didn't know that," said Emperor Nurbison, yawning as if he weren't very interested. Really, he was very interested indeed.

"Got her from a wizard when I was a girl," said Veronica. "He gave her enchanted hair. When the rays of the full moon touch the hair, she comes to life for a year and a day. But when she does, oh! She just

talks about her hair. All the time. Just
blabbers on and on and on. Soon learned
to keep her out of the moonlight, I can
tell you. She's called Miss Dolly-Chops,
or something. Only kept her on display
because I knew she frightened you."

Old Empress Veronica tossed the picture and the doll back in the cupboard.

"Beloved Mother," said Nurbison, "Empress of my heart. Why don't you sit back in your chair and rest those knees of yours while I put the cookies back in the kitchen?"

INNOCENT WHISTLING

"I know what you're up to," said
Veronica. "Sneaking an extra cookie. Try and
there'll be trouble, young man."

"Mother, I promise I shall not steal a
single cookie."

I'm not lying, thought Nurbison. *I'm not
going to steal any cookies at all. I'm going to
steal something else.*

Once he was sure his mom wasn't
looking, the emperor eased open the
cupboard door, hoping it wouldn't creak. He
found the doll and stuffed it inside his cloak.
Big, swirling cloaks are just the best for
hiding stuff you've swiped.

Yes, this magic doll will be very useful,
thought Emperor Nurbison. *Very useful indeed.
I feel a plan forming in my evil-genius brain.*

He didn't dare say "Foo hoo hoo hoo" in case his mother figured out he was up to something. So he wrote it down on a piece of paper, looked at it, smiled, then ate the paper. It was tastier than the cookie.

A Month Later

It was a month later.

King Edwin sat on his throne, picking scabs off his knees. It had been three whole days since King Edwin's last amazing invention—the skateboard. He made two of them, so Shark Boy and

Thundercloud could have one each. But he hadn't invented knee pads yet.

Something was strange. Minister Jill wasn't telling him to stop picking.

"Jill? You're forgetting to say, 'Leave the scabs on; they help your skin to heal.' I could say it for you if you like. Oh wait, I just did."

"I'm not really thinking about your

scabs, Edwin—I'm thinking about Emperor Nurbison. He's been acting a bit odd."

That was true. Three weeks before, he had marched up to the dotted line between Edwinland and Nurbisonia, and instead of calling Centurion Alisha a foolish fool, or just invading, he'd said:

A few days after that, the emperor had started wearing a big yellow daisy in his crown. Then he'd let his peasants have a proper bath. Which was strange, because normally the emperor loved his peasants to be filthy and miserable and made them wash their hair with slug juice and brush their teeth with dog sweat.

"There's just something peculiar about it all," said Minister Jill.

A palace guard suddenly popped out of a trapdoor in the floor. There were so many trapdoors and secret passages in Edwin's castle that it was a wonder there was any space left for actual rooms.

"Your Majesty! Minister Jill! The *Nurbisonia Times*. Just delivered. One copy for each of you."

Jill and Edwin looked at each other in amazement. Nurbisonia had a newspaper now? The evil emperor was letting people *read*?

First, Jill made herself a big cup of coffee. Most grown-ups need coffee five times a day or they turn into zombies. Just ask them.

Then Jill sat down with the paper. The front page had some very big news.

Jill flicked to the next page.

Nurbisonia Times

4TH OF OCTEBRUARY ⟶ PRICE: 2 BRONZE BITS

"I'M NICE NOW!"

- BIG CHANGE FOR THE NOT-SO-EVIL EMPEROR
- FULL STORY: PAGES 1, 2, 3, 4, 5, 6, 7, 8, 9, 10, 11, 12, 13, 14, 15, 16, 17, 18

A NEW NURBISON?

THE BIG INTERVIEW

BY OUR CHIEF REPORTER

After years of being popular and strong and handsome (but also utterly evil), it seems our great emperor's had a change of heart about the whole "evil" thing. We caught up with him in his stunning castle penthouse to find out more...

THE TIMES: So! Emperor Nurbison, Earl of

Unjerland, Overlord of Glenth and Boolander . . .

EMPEROR NURBISON: (waving his hand) Oh, you don't have to call me by those fancy titles every time. I see myself as a . . . how do people say it? A "regular guy."

THE TIMES: I'll tell you what else people are saying . . . "Emperor, why the big change?"

EMPEROR: I'm so glad you asked me that. I used to be very evil indeed. Then I was defeated twice in a row by my delightful neighbor King Edwin Flashypants. Wonderful little chap, love him to death. So I thought to myself: Why does he keep winning? Is good better than evil after all?

On that day, I decided to become a nice emperor. **FOO HOO**— Oh, sorry. That was my old evil laugh. You won't be hearing that anymore. I've got a new, jolly laugh now. SQUEE HEE HEE HEE! Like it?

THE TIMES: I do. SQUEE HEE HEE HEE! Wow, it's very catchy.

THE ~~EVIL~~ HANDSOME EMPEROR RELAXES IN HIS DEEPLY ~~SINISTER~~ NICE HOME.

EMPEROR: And I won't stop there. In my evil years I caused a lot of misery. From now on, I'll spread all the happiness I can. I'm becoming a toymaker. I'm turning the castle into a big toy factory. I'll sell the toys in my new toy shops, and with luck . . . where I once brought sadness . . . I can bring a little bit of joy. *Sniff.*

EDITOR'S NOTE: AT THIS MOMENT, A TEAR REALLY DID RUN DOWN OUR EMPEROR'S BEAUTIFUL FACE!

THE TIMES: Good luck, Emperor. We can't wait for the first shop to open!

"What do you make of all that?" said Minister Jill to King Edwin.

"Make of what?" said Edwin. "The news? Oh, I don't look at news; it's never fun. But there are comic strips at the back—look. This one's called Mister Poo, and it's about a poo who lives in a house made of poo! You'd enjoy it, Jill. The jokes are very clever."

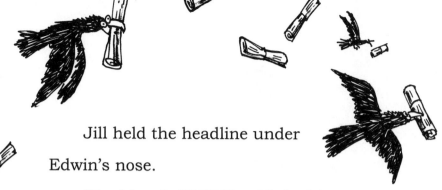

Jill held the headline under Edwin's nose.

"Nurbison's NICE?" said the king. "That IS big news. Why did they hide it on the front page?"

All of a sudden, the sky went dark. There was a thundering sound on the roof, like the heaviest rain King Edwin had ever heard.

But it wasn't rain.

"Newspapers!" said Jill.

High above Edwinland, hundreds of the emperor's crows were dropping copies of the *Nurbisonia Times*. Everybody in Edwinland picked one up and read it.

Seconds later, Megan the Jester burst

into the throne room. She pulled off her

Thundercloud hat and cape.

"Have you seen it? Have you? Have you seen it? Have you seen it? Have you? Have you seen it? Have you? Have you? Have you seen it?" said Megan, breathless. "The emperor's going to make toys! So many toys. I love toys! Can we go to the toy shop as soon as it opens? *Please?* **Please?**"

When people get older, most of them forget how cool toys are. That's just one of the things that makes grown-ups more boring than kids. But even though she was a grown-up, Megan never forgot, and Edwin loved her for it.

"Well, Emperor Nurbison *is* good now, I suppose . . . ," said Edwin.

"He's pretended to be nice before,

then turned out to be horrible," said Jill. "But he never pretended for more than an hour. If it seems like he's been good for a whole month—maybe he really *is* good. *Maybe.* We'd better give him a chance, at least."

"Megan," said King Edwin, "we'll go to the toy shop."

"Hooray! Yay! Whoo-hoo! All the other words like that!" said Megan. Then she ran upstairs to see how much was in her piggy bank.

Megan forgot to pick up her Thundercloud cape, thought King Edwin. *And the helmet got a bit bashed up when she dropped it. But I know she loves it, so I'll find some tape and fix it for her.*

He picked up the newspaper and looked at the comic strips again. Mister Poo was wearing poo for a hat and walking his pet poo, when he tripped over a poo and fell in some poo. It was just the kind of thing Edwin liked. But he wasn't laughing as much as he normally would.

Something was worrying him about Megan. But what was it?

51

Grand Opening

For the next few nights, Nurbison's
peasants hammered and sawed and
built, saying things like "Let's lay some
bricks here" and "Where shall I put the
floorboards?" and "On the floor, dummy."
In just a few days, there was a shiny new

toy shop at the edge of Nurbisonia, just by the dotted line.

The crows flapped over Edwinland again, dropping paper scrolls that said:

EMPEROR NURBISON'S **TOY** SUPERSTORE

GRAND OPENING: SATURDAY, 12 NOON

"A GREAT BIG FUN SANDWICH OF A SHOP!"

Before the sun even rose on Saturday morning, King Edwin Flashypants was woken by a great big jester trampolining on his bed.

"Let's be first in line!" said Megan. "Let's! Let's! Let's!"

But when they got there, a great snaking line of people was already in front of the superstore. The people of Edwinland couldn't wait to see what was inside.

"Your Majesty! You should come to the front of the line," said one peasant.

"You are the king, after all," said another.

"Thanks, but I think I'll wait like everyone else," said King Edwin. "Just because I'm royal doesn't mean I should jump the line."

When she heard this, Minister Jill felt incredibly proud. She turned to tell Edwin he was growing into a very wise and mature king, but Edwin had already started a booger-flicking contest with some other children.

All morning, the people waited. The sun crept across

10 POINTS

the sky, stayed
still for a bit
just to annoy
everyone, then
crept a little more.

"Hey, Megan," said King Edwin. "Let's pretend there's a dinosaur, which is also a zombie and also a Dracula. A dino-zomb-cula! And it's attacking this line! But wait, here come Thundercloud and Shark Boy!"

Megan didn't even look his way.

"Megan? Megan. Megan. Megan. Megany-Megan. *Megaaaaaaaaaaaaaaaan.*"

"I wonder if they do a discount for jesters?" said Megan, gazing at the superstore.

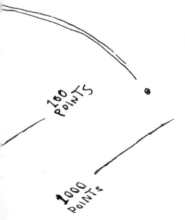

At seven seconds before twelve, Globulus popped out of a hatch on top of the shop.

"I kind of like, you know, sort of, declare this superstore kind of open, sort of thing!" said Globulus.

That meant the superstore was open.

Everybody hurried inside. The shop was simply enormous. The shelves seemed to go on forever. But wherever he walked, Edwin noticed the toys had one thing in common.

"They're all Emperor Nurbison dolls," he said.

"I know!" said Megan. "And so many different kinds!"

NURBISON
CLASSIC

DEEP-SEA DIVER
NURBISON

CHEF NURBISON

FUNKALICIOUS
NURBISON

She was right.

BURGER AND
FRIES NURBISON

COWGIRL
NURBISON

RETIARIUS
GLADIATOR
NURBISON

NANNY
NURBISON

And lots and lots more.

Hundreds of different Nurbisons.

EXPLORER
NURBISON

PRINCESS
NURBISON

For boys who thought buying a doll wasn't for them, there was another part of the shop where they sold all the same stuff, but under a big sign that said ACTION FIGURES.

"Nurbison is such a bighead!" said King Edwin, who was secretly a bit jealous he hadn't been the first to think of making dolls of himself.

Megan chose a Princess Nurbison doll and followed the THIS WAY TO PAY signs. Emperor Nurbison worked the giant cash register, which played jolly pipe music whenever he made a sale.

"Such merriment! Enjoy your toys, everyone!" said the emperor. "Oh, hello, King Edwin, so glad you could come! SQUEE HEE HEE HEE!"

After banging the register's huge buttons for a while, the emperor announced his arms were tired. "But

never mind!" he said. "One of my sinister—I mean, *un*-sinister—soldiers will take over."

Nurbison and Globulus stepped out the back door. The moment they were alone, the emperor's smile collapsed into a scowl.

"It's infernally hard work, pretending to be good," said Nurbison. "I've never kept it up for this long before. And this false beard is giving me a rash."

The emperor pulled a fake beard from his chin. He'd had a shave. *In secret.*

"Just, you know, a few more days, Your Sensationalness," said Globulus, slapping moisturizer on the emperor's bare face.

"Yes!" said Nurbison. "And then all shall know the true might of the Evil Emperor Nurbison!"

Then the emperor had to fetch a mop and bucket, because a baby had just been sick in aisle five.

Big Pouty Face

Bang, bang, bang. Bang, bang. Ba-ba-bang. Bang. Ba-bang. Bang, bang, bang, ba-ba-ba-ba-ba-bang.

Bang, bang. Ba-bang.

Ba-bangbangbangbangbangbang.

Bang.

Shark Boy was knocking on
Thundercloud's bedroom door.

Edwin had just put a cool tail on the
Shark Boy hat. It took lots and lots of tape
to keep it in place, and he was very proud
of it.

"Megan! My lessons are over! Let's
play superheroes! *Megaaaaan!*"

There was no reply.
Edwin jumped onto
a giant boingy spring.
Giant boingy springs were
another cool way to get
around inside the castle. The
spring boinged him all the
way up to the battlements.

He gazed across
Edwinland. It seemed like
everybody was carrying
Emperor Nurbison dolls.

And there was Megan, by
the castle moat. It looked like
playing superheroes couldn't be
further from her mind. Edwin
frowned as he watched her

dancing her Princess Nurbison all around
and singing a song to it. Something like this:

Here's a little ditty

To tell you you're so pretty.

A princess with a silky beard so fine.

You really are so nice

And at such a modest price—

You retailed for just seven ninety-nine.

King Edwin called Centurion Alisha. She clanked toward him in her steel armor, then stamped her feet so hard that a chunk of the ceiling shook loose in the room below and hit Minister Jill on the head.

"Your Majesty!" said Centurion Alisha.

"Alisha? If anybody needs me, I'll be in my throne room having a massive sulk," said Edwin.

Kings never have small sulks. Edwin really threw himself into this one, doing all the things nine-year-olds do when they're in a bad mood.

He pouted until his face got tired.

He sat on his throne the wrong way around with his feet sticking in the air.

He pouted some more.

He kicked his foot with his other foot.

He moaned and sighed and banged things with a stick.

It's not fair, he thought. *Megan is my best friend, and she doesn't want to play superheroes with me anymore. She just wants to play with her stupid Nurbison doll like everybody else.*

Normally, Megan would be there to cheer Edwin up when he was like this. But today, Megan was the reason *why* he was like this.

In came Minister Jill, rubbing the bump on her head.

"Something's wrong about all this," said Jill.

"Mumble mumble mumble," mumbled Edwin, because when you're mega-moody it's important to speak like that.

"We've let Emperor Nurbison sell toys

to everyone in Edwinland," Jill continued. "And it's good that we did, because we said we'd give him a chance to be nice . . ."

Minister Jill took a deep breath, then puffed her cheeks out.

Edwin checked the list of Jill's moves he kept under his throne pillow. Puffy cheeks meant that Jill's next word would be *but.*

"But," said Jill, "just say he *wasn't* nice. Then the toys could be part of some new plan of—well, how can I say this—*not-niceness.*"

Just then, Megan bounced into the throne room, and the wind blew a hundred new toy catalogs through the door after her. Nurbison's crows had been dropping them for the last hour. They fell so thick in some places that the shorter peasants were stuck up to their necks.

"There's a new Princess Nurbison play set!" Megan gasped. "It's got an ice-cream parlor and a beard salon—look!"

She held two catalogs in front of King Edwin's face, one for each eye. Then Megan the Jester ran up to her bedroom, grabbed

some gold coins from her piggy bank, and dashed out to the superstore.

"Maybe we should take a really close look at a Nurbison doll," said Minister Jill. "Even though I'm absolutely sure there's nothing to worry about."

"Oh, I know where to find one of those," said King Edwin.

And he climbed the stairs.

All the way to Megan's bedroom.

Find the Princess

As he pushed open Megan's bedroom door, Edwin thought, *I'm just borrowing her doll, not stealing it. And while I know that's not quite true, if I keep saying it in my head, I might start to believe it. I'm*

borrowing, not stealing.
Borrowing, not stealing.

Since the last time
Edwin was in Megan's
room, she had built a
giant play castle on the
floor out of old toys and
games. The Princess
Nurbison doll was
perched right on top.

Wow. You could stack seven of me up alongside that thing, thought Edwin. *Hey! If I had six identical brothers, you really could stack up seven of me, and we could be a circus act. The Flying Flashypants-es! And we'd wear spangly catsuits and we'd flip into the big top like this . . .*

King Edwin tried a cartwheel, stabbed his left hand with his crown, tumbled to the floor, and nudged the play castle.

It creaked and rocked—but it didn't come crashing down on Edwin.

That really **wobbled** *a lot then,* thought Edwin. *But it didn't ACTUALLY come crashing down on my head, so I reckon it's totally safe to climb.*

Edwin clambered up the princess's castle. When he couldn't find the next handhold, he opened up board games and looked for useful things inside the boxes. Hooky Duck had a tiny fishing rod. With a bit of hook-throwing and bit of reel-winding, Edwin climbed higher still.

At the top, the king grabbed the

princess doll with his teeth and climbed all the way down again.

Whew! Not so hard, thought Edwin, leaning against the play castle's biggest tower.

The castle groaned, rumbled, and toppled over.

Edwin ran.

I'm not going to get crushed, he thought. *Going to make it to the door . . . just in time . . .*

Just . . . in . . . time . . .

Seventy jigsaw puzzles landed on his head. Alisha and the palace guards had to use every single rod from Hooky Duck to pull him out.

Later, down in the throne room, Jill and Edwin looked at the Princess Nurbison doll this way, then that way. Then sideways, topways, and underways.

"Just a normal-looking doll," said Edwin.

"Well, nothing weird about the outside," said Jill. "So maybe there's something *inside* it."

King Edwin was still pretty sure Emperor Nurbison was nice these days. *But if he isn't,* Edwin thought, *what might he hide inside a doll . . . ?*

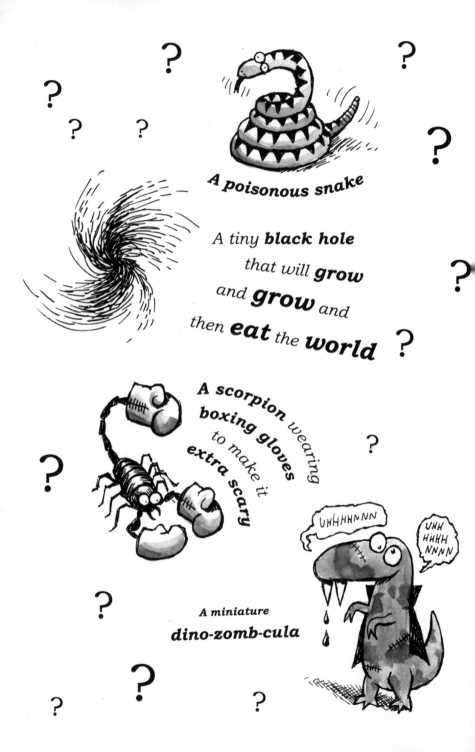

Just the thought of that last one made Edwin's blood run cold.

"We have to open it up and find out," said King Edwin. "Jill? The big tongs, please."

Jill fetched a couple of pairs of tongs from the fireplace. Edwin gripped Princess Nurbison's head with one pair, and Jill held Princess Nurbison's feet with the other.

Megan really, really, really, really wouldn't like this, thought Edwin. *But if I fix the doll straight afterward, she'll never know.*

"One, two—" said Jill.

"Wait," said Edwin. "Let's count down, not up. Down sounds cooler."

"Oh, all right then," said Minister Jill.

"Three, two, one—**pull!**"

They both heaved. With a pop, then a rip, the Princess Nurbison doll broke in two.

Edwin and Jill each looked at their own part.

"Just wood and wire and cotton stuffing in my half," said Jill.

"Same here," said Edwin.

"WHAT HAVE YOU DONE?!"

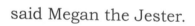

said Megan the Jester.

Jill and Edwin looked up. There she was, clutching her new Princess Nurbison play set. They hadn't heard her come in.

"You've broken Princess Nurbison! You rotten snot-lords, you snapped her in half!"

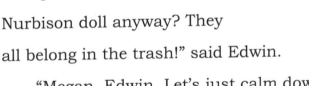

"Well—well—who cares about a stupid Princess Nurbison doll anyway? They all belong in the trash!" said Edwin.

"Megan, Edwin. Let's just calm down," said Minister Jill, "before we all say a lot of angry words we won't be proud of later."

But Edwin and Megan weren't listening. They were too busy saying lots of angry words they wouldn't be proud of later.

"*I* care!" said Megan. "She was my favorite toy, and you're just jealous because . . . because . . . because . . .

YOUR SUPERHERO COSTUMES ARE GARBAGE!"

"They are not!" said King Edwin.

"They are so!" said Megan. "They're not even made properly—they've got lots of tape

hanging off them and it gets stuck to my hair!"

The Thundercloud helmet was on the floor. Megan kicked it hard. It flew out the window and landed in the castle's cardboard recycling bin.

"Edwin! Megan! Calm down," said Minister Jill. She knew perfectly well that she couldn't say anything to help now, but all ministers know it's good to be seen doing *something*, even when it's totally and utterly pointless.

"Well I . . . well I . . . well I don't care if you don't want to play superheroes anymore because you're a **rotten jester** anyway!" said Edwin.

"And you're a **rotten king!** The WORST EVER!" said Megan.

"Well, you're a MASSIVE STINKY BUTTFACE!" said King Edwin Flashypants.

"No! You're the

MASSIVE STINKY BUTTFACE!"

said Megan.

Once people have called each other massive stinky buttfaces, there's really nothing more they can say.

Trying not to cry, Megan ran to the kitchen and gathered a loaf of bread and a hunk of cheese into a huge polka-dotted handkerchief. She tied the hankie to a stick and stomped to the castle gate.

"Megan, wait. All we were doing was—" said Jill.

"I'm leaving Edwinland forever! Goodbye, **dolly murderers!**"

Megan slammed the gate of Edwin's castle so hard that the shock wave knocked peasants into ditches half a mile away.

And then Megan the Jester, who had been

King Edwin's faithful friend since he was a little boy, was gone.

Edwin ran to his bedroom.

He didn't want to speak to anyone.

Jill picked up the top half of the doll.

Peculiar, she thought. *The emperor could have just painted that beard on. Nobody would have minded. But it's made of lots of very small black hairs.*

Very, very peculiar.

Hairy Magic

That night, Nurbison and Globulus climbed the steepest, most winding staircase in the emperor's castle. Flaming torches on the walls lit their way with a bright, steady glow.

"Oh, that's not right at all," said the emperor. "Change the setting, Globulus!"

Globulus found a knob on the wall.
He clicked it around from "Bright, Steady
Glow" to "Dim, Spooky Flicker."

"Much better," said the emperor, and
he continued up the stairs, stumbling
a few times because he
could hardly see
the steps now.

"Erm, Emperor?"
said Globulus.

"You're not about to ask for something, are you, Globulus?" said Nurbison. "You know very well that I only let you ask for something every five years."

Emperor Nurbison pulled a little diary from his cloak and flicked back through the pages.

"Oh!" said the emperor, his evil eyebrow arching. "Five years, two months, and three days ago: 'Globulus asks His Imperial Greatness to pass the ketchup.' So you really *are* due for another. Let's get it over with, then."

"It's um, kind of, you know, it's this," said Globulus. "There's, like, thousands of dolls of you in Edwinland now. But there's, kind of, no dolls to be helpers to

them dolls. To keep all the emperor dolls company. Might be nice, yeah? Helper dolls. Sort of thing."

"Are you talking about making *Globulus* toys?" said Emperor Nurbison. "Ha! Why would anybody in the world want a toy of *you*? Oh, Globulus, you are funny sometimes. You make me 'foo hoo hoo hoo,' you really do."

Globulus knew the emperor liked his laugh to echo in a frightening way if they were on a stone staircase, so—with a sigh—he turned up the echo knob on the wall.

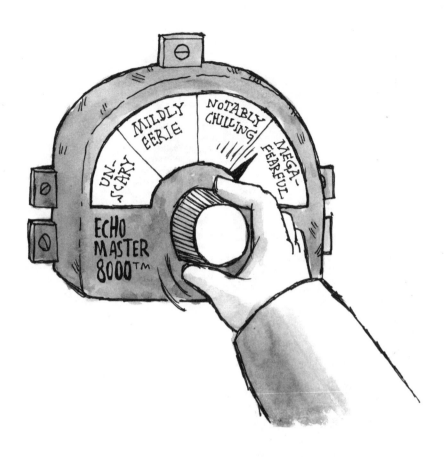

At last they came to a chamber at the top of the tower. Below a huge window was a tiny chair. And in the chair sat Miss Dolly-Chops, the stolen magical doll.

Half the hair was missing from her head.

"It took ages to cut off tiny bits of her magic hair, then stick them to the chins of all those dolls," said the emperor. "Used up all the glue sticks in my crafting box. But oh, it was worth it. For tonight, the moon shall be full! If my calculations are correct, Globulus—and I did once get a gold star

for Evil Math at school, so they should
be—the moon will rise over those hills
precisely . . . now!"

Emperor Nurbison and Globulus
waited. No moon.

"Precisely . . . now!" said the emperor
again. Still no moon.

Then the emperor remembered the
clocks had been turned back a couple of days
before, so moonrise would be an hour later.

Nurbison and Globulus went
downstairs and played some table tennis
for a bit, then came up again.

"AS I WAS SAYING," said the emperor.
"The full moon shall rise over those
hills exactly, definitely, and precisely . . .

NOW!"

The chalky white circle glided over the horizon. Its cold, moony beams touched the enchanted hair of Miss Dolly-Chops.

The hair began to gleam with a dazzling black light. I bet you've never seen a ray of dazzling black light before. Neither had the emperor or Globulus.

"Kind of totally wow and all of that!" said Globulus.

Miss Dolly-Chops sat up.

"I am Miss Dolly-Chops!" she said in a voice that tinkled like a mountain stream.

"It's alive, it's alive!" said Emperor Nurbison. "The magic hair really works! Hair that I have stolen for my evil plans.

FOO HOO HOO HOO!"

"But how? My stunning locks are all here on my dainty—"

She touched her stubbly head.

"AAAAAAHHHH! MY HAAIIRRR!" said Miss Dolly-Chops.

"Half of it's over there in Edwinland, my dear. On the chins of a thousand dolls. Mixed with a little bit of hair from someone else."

The emperor pulled off his false beard and stroked his bare face.

"And *that* hair will give them a certain personality . . . **FOO HOO HOO!**"

Back in Edwinland, lit by the full moon, the toys came to life.

"I am Nurbison!" said one.

"I am Nurbison!" said another.

And all across the kingdom, the cry went up.

"I am Nurbison . . .

I am Nurbison . . .

We are Nurbison!

WE ARE
NURBISON!

WE ARE
NURBISON!"

So ... Many ... Nurbisons ...

All that night, King Edwin Flashypants tossed and turned. He couldn't stop thinking about Megan. He was still angry with her,

but he was beginning to feel bad about the things he had said. And he was very sad that she had gone.

Well, this is a new mood, he thought. *I've never felt quite this way before. I should give it a name, like "angry-sorry." Or "guilty-grumps" or "whoops-grrr."*

When he finally got to sleep, he had a bad dream. He dreamed that Emperor Nurbison was standing on his chest, except Nurbison looked like an angry crossing guard.

When Edwin woke up, there was an angry Crossing Guard Nurbison doll standing on his chest.

The king pinched himself to make sure he was really awake. Ouch! Yes, he was.

"Your kingdom belongs to Nurbison!" said the figure. It jabbed Edwin on the nose with the sharp end of the stop sign, just to prove the point.

It was true. The magical toys had
seized Edwinland while everyone slept.
Centurion Alisha had put up a fight.

The trouble was, she had bought more Nurbison dolls than anyone. A Matador Nurbison pulled down her helmet while a Ninja Nurbison grabbed her sword. Then a Wrestler Nurbison stamped on her toes and tripped her. There were so many dolls that there was nothing anyone could do to stop them.

Edwinland had only one village. It was called Village. And soon, an army of dolls paraded Edwin and Jill around it.

"Here is your king! Here is your minister!" bellowed an Explorer Nurbison to a crowd of peasants. "They rule no more!"

"So I suppose Emperor Nurbison had an evil plan after all," said Edwin. "Probably something to do with the dolls being magic."

"Probably that, yes," said Minister Jill with a sigh.

Just then, the real, life-size Emperor Nurbison strode into Village. He walked very quickly, because he had written a brand-new and much faster striding theme for the marching band who followed him. The old striding theme had gotten only a two-star review in *Evil Ruler Monthly* magazine. Nurbison fumed for a whole week.

The emperor suddenly stopped striding—which caught the band by surprise. They all piled up behind him. Trombones crunched into banjos, which barged into bagpipes. The sound was like a whale chewing a mouthful of tin cans and fart cushions.

"Idiots of Edwinland!" said the
emperor. "You really believed that I had
turned into a nice man selling lovely toys!
All part of my wicked game, of course.
With magic hair from my magic doll, and
just a sprinkle of hair
from my own beautiful

face, I knew the toys would come to life as little versions of me. Just as nasty! Just as cruel! Just as keen to seize Edwinland!

FOO HOO HOO HOO!"

All the dolls "Foo hoo hoo hooed" with him.

"You have done well, dolls. But I'm here now, so *I'm* in charge. First, make me a huge ice throne from the frozen tears of my enemies. Then bring me an eighteen-inch pizza with a topping of roasted baby seals. And then—"

A Beekeeper Nurbison stepped forward.

"But I am in charge! Because I am Nurbison!" he said.

"No, *I* am in charge, for *I* am Nurbison!" said a Clown Nurbison.

Too late, the real Emperor Nurbison saw his mistake. Yes, all the toys wanted to take over Edwinland because they had the emperor's personality. He'd gotten that much right. But he'd missed something. Because they had his personality, every single toy wanted to be the boss.

A mob of dolls knocked the real emperor to the dusty ground.

"I am on the dusty ground!" croaked Emperor Nurbison, spitting out dust from his dusty mouth. "How dare you! I am your master, you horrid dolls!"

"Horrid *action figures*," said a Special Forces Soldier Nurbison.

"Silence!" said a Strongman Nurbison. "Now hear this! I will rule you all because I am the strongest. The clue is in the name. Strong . . . man. Strongman."

Wrestler Nurbison punched Strongman Nurbison into a hedge.

"No! I shall rule!" said the wrestler.

"I hardly think so," said a voice as sweet as the sprinkles on a birthday cake.

Megan's Princess Nurbison bounced forward. She was still in two pieces, but both halves of her had come to life in the night.

She fought the wrestler. Because she was in two parts, she could poke him in the eye and kick him in the butt all at the same time. And the wrestler was no match for her Pointy-Hat Attack.

"*I* shall rule!" she said. "Anyone have a problem with that?"

"Er, yeah, I do," said Globulus. "There's only one proper emperor here, and he's, you know, had a lot of experience on the job, so—"

The princess booted Globulus, who landed on a compost heap.

"All hail Princess Nurbison!" shouted the toys. "ALL HAIL PRINCESS NURBISON!"

Far away, beyond Edwinland and Nurbisonia, in the jungle of Lim-Bloo-Bloo-Bloo-Bloo-Bloo-Bloo-Bloo, Megan the Jester sat on a log. She'd been walking all night in jester shoes, and her feet were tired. Jester shoes are made for prancing, not walking.

She couldn't find a name for the way she felt, but it was a lot like "angry-sorry," and quite "whoops-grrrr," with just a touch of "guilty-grumps." It was bad of Edwin and Jill to break her doll, but Megan had thought about it for a while now, and she'd realized they wouldn't have done it without a good reason. But Megan had been so furious that she hadn't asked what that reason was.

And now I've left Edwinland, she thought. *I've nobody to jest at. If I can't be a jester, I just don't know who I am.*

A little lizard scuttled across the log. Megan had an idea.

"I'll be your jester, Lady Lizard of Lim-Bloo-Bloo-Bloo-Bloo-Bloo-Bloo-Bloo! Let the amusements begin!"

Megan strummed her lute and told jokes that she thought a reptile might get.

Q: What do you call a lizard who goes moo?
A: *A cow-meleon!*
Q: What kind of snake is good at math?
A: *An adder!*

Q: Doctor, doctor! I keep thinking I'm a boa constrictor.

A: *You can't get around me like that, you know.*

The lizard blinked.

Then it pitter-pattered away into the trees.

"Oh dear, oh dear," said Megan. "What shall become of me?"

She picked up her stick and handkerchief, and on she walked. But with a little bit of a sniff. And a little bit of a tear.

Teamwork

"She keeps saying 'Foo hoo hoo hoo!' That's *my* evil laugh!"

The emperor spun around. Edwin, Jill,

and Globulus ducked to avoid the drops of water that flew from Nurbison's fingertips.

Evil emperors never dry their hands properly after going to the bathroom.

"She stole it from me! That's just evil! And being evil is fantastic—I'm not saying it isn't—but . . . Oh, you know what I mean!"

The four of them had been locked in King Edwin's bedroom for ages, while Princess Nurbison decided what to do with them.

"But we've got lots of games," said Edwin. "We've got travel chess, giant chess, and chess. I don't like being locked up either, but at least my room's a fun place to be locked up."

"No, no, no, no, no, no!" said the emperor. "It's *my* room, just like this is *my* castle. I claim all of Edwinland. Haven't you learned that by now?"

Edwin put his superhero helmet on.

Nurbison pulled the helmet off and hurled it away. Some ends

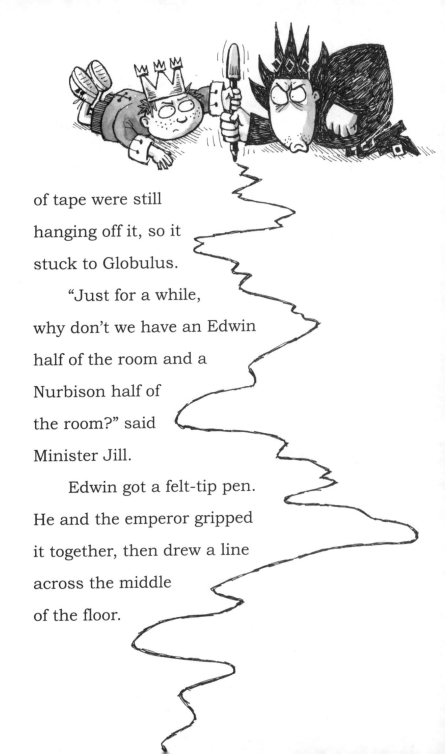

of tape were still
hanging off it, so it
stuck to Globulus.

"Just for a while,
why don't we have an Edwin
half of the room and a
Nurbison half of
the room?" said
Minister Jill.

Edwin got a felt-tip pen.
He and the emperor gripped
it together, then drew a line
across the middle
of the floor.

Both of them kept trying to push the pen to make their half bigger, so the line wobbled and zigzagged across the wooden boards.

"Oh, we're both being silly," said Edwin. "Here we are squabbling, when evil toys have taken over *both* our kingdoms. Maybe we should work together to get rid of them."

"What a horrible day this is," said the emperor. "First my enchanted dolls turn against me, then I'm locked in a bedroom, then I find myself thinking, *King Edwin's right*."

"Your Majesty? A private word," said Minister Jill. She and Edwin went into Edwin's old playhouse. It was toddler-size,

but it was
better than
nothing.

"Work
with the evil
emperor?"
whispered
Jill. "Who is *definitely* still evil? Are you
quite sure, Edwin?"

"Totally sure. Mostly sure. A bit
sure," said Edwin. "But you have to admit
he can be very clever. We could use his
brains at the moment."

Edwin and Jill stepped out of the
playhouse. Nurbison and Globulus
jumped back, pretending they hadn't been
listening at the door.

Edwin held out his hand.

Nurbison shook it.

It was the olden days, and cameras hadn't been invented yet. So Globulus drew a very good picture of this historic moment.

"Erm, sort of, hooray, type of thing!" said Globulus.

Soon Jill stood at Edwin's chalkboard, chalk in hand. At the top of the board, she wrote:

"Righty ho!" said Jill. "We need some ideas. Let's get creative."

King Edwin put up his hand and said, "I've got one. What about if we—"

"No," said Emperor Nurbison.

"Okay then," said Edwin. "Let's see if we can—"

"No," said Nurbison.

"Then what about—"

"No."

"Or we could—"

"No."

"We could try to—"

"No."

"Or let's—"

"No."

"Emperor, really," said Jill. "How do you know if the ideas are good or bad before you've even heard them?"

The emperor looked at her like she was being very silly indeed.

"How can they be good ideas if it wasn't me who thought them up?" he said.

"We're going to hear each other's ideas, no matter how daft they might seem," insisted Jill.

Globulus put up his hand.

"We could, like, trap all the toys in my hat," he said.

You couldn't even fit one doll in Globulus's hat, never mind thousands.

It really was the worst idea Jill had ever heard. But she had to play by her own rules, so she wrote it on the chalkboard.

Hours passed. The board filled up with ideas, ideas, and more ideas. But deep down, Jill knew none of them would work.

Then Emperor Nurbison noticed something. There was still a little strip of tape stuck to Globulus's nose.

Because tape is almost see-through, nobody had spotted it.

"Wait, you've got tape!" said the emperor. "That's useful for loads of things. Let's think about tape."

Edwin ran to his superhero-costume-making table and found two rolls of tape.

"Minister Jill? Please wipe the board clean!" said King Edwin. "I think we've just had the idea. Not *an* idea. *The* idea."

A few minutes later, Jill banged on the locked bedroom door.

"What?" said the Ninja Nurbison doll on the other side.

"We request an audience with Her Majesty Princess Nurbison," said the minister.

The Princess Will See You Now

King Edwin, Emperor Nurbison, Minister Jill, and Globulus walked into the throne room. A sea of Nurbison doll faces glared back at them.

Both halves of Princess Nurbison sat on Edwin's throne.

"Greetings, fools!" said the princess. "Have you met my future wife?"

Next to the princess was a scared-looking Miss Dolly-Chops.

"That's right! We're getting married," said the princess. "And yes, two lady dolls can get married. This is the modern world. Get used to it. Now, feeble rulers of yesteryear, what do you want?"

"We wish to proclaim you the rightful ruler of these lands," said Edwin. "Edwinland and Nurbisonia are yours forever."

"So we came to hand you our precious crowns," said the emperor.

He and Edwin took the crowns from their heads.

"All dolls in the room should make sure to get a really good look. You'll definitely want to laugh at us," said Edwin.

"Indeed," said the emperor. "So—and this is just an idea—you should probably form two lines. Two very long, very straight lines."

"Dolls? Form two lines!" said the princess.

"And if they stood on tall stools they'd get a really good view," said Edwin.

"Yes, stools!" said the emperor. "Such a good idea from a child wise beyond his years."

said the princess.

Frightened peasants fetched stools for the dolls.

"And now," said the princess, "bring me the crowns."

Slowly, very slowly, Edwin and Emperor Nurbison shuffled down the middle of the hall, between the two lines of dolls—who chuckled a deep "foo hoo hoo hoo." They were so busy "foo hoo hooing" at the king and the emperor that there was something they didn't spot.

Long pieces of tape trailed from the crowns. The two bits of tape went all the way back to Globulus and Jill, who each had a roll spinning on a finger.

"Why are you walking so slowly? Get a move on!" said Princess Nurbison. But the king and the emperor couldn't risk speeding up. If the tape broke or fell off, the whole plan would be ruined.

As they neared the throne, the princess narrowed her eyes.

"Wait a minute," she said. "What's that stuck to the crowns? Is it . . . tape? What are you trying to—"

"Now!" said Edwin.

The king jumped to the left. The emperor jumped to the right. They pressed

those long trails of tape up against the chins
of the dolls.

"Mmmffmmmmmnnpphh!" said a
surprised Ballerina Nurbison through the tape.

"Mmgrrrmmph!" said a Jockey
Nurbison.

"**Mmmmrrrgrrmmph!**" said a Sailor Nurbison.

"**Grmmphmmph!**" said a Funkalicious Nurbison.

You get the idea.

"And . . . throw!" said Edwin.

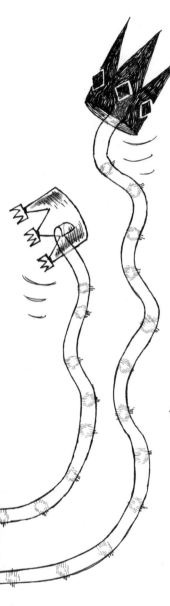

He and the emperor flung their crowns high in the air . . . RIPPING away the tape from the dolls' chins and taking all the enchanted hair with them. The Nurbison dolls flopped to the ground.

Without their magic beards, they were just ordinary dolls again.

All except the one on the throne.

"You destroyed my army!" screamed Princess Nurbison. "Now you shall feel my anger! **KUNG-FU ATTACK!**"

The princess's hands and feet were a blur as both halves of her jabbed and pummeled Edwin, Emperor Nurbison, Jill, and Globulus into a corner of the throne room.

"POINTY-HAT ATTACK!" said Princess Nurbison, backing into the opposite corner so she would build up some speed.

Oh no, thought Edwin. *I've seen her do this on the dolls, and they've got wooden heads. What will it do to a human being?*

The princess ran, then jumped. Her top half hurtled through the air—straight toward King Edwin's head.

I'm finished, thought King Edwin.

"You're finished," said the emperor. "Still, better you than me, eh?"

But just as the pointy hat was about to strike Edwin's face, it stopped. In midair. Gripped by a powerful hand.

The hand of a hero.

"NOBODY hurts Shark Boy! Not when Thundercloud's around!"

Megan! There she was, wearing her Thundercloud helmet. She'd rescued it from the cardboard recycling bin, so there were loads of rotten banana peels stuck to it. No matter how many times Jill asked, people always threw the rubbish in the wrong bin. But stinky banana peels or not, Edwin couldn't have been happier to see her.

"You came back!" said Edwin. "What happened, you see, is the toys all had magic hair in their beards, and they came to life and took over, and Emperor Nurbison thought they would obey him but they didn't, and then— Hey, how about I tell you the whole thing later, after we've won? If we win. Let's try to win first."

"Let me go! LET ME GO!" the princess yelled.

Megan was holding the top half of the princess like an ice-cream cone, but an ice-cream cone with fists and snapping teeth. Meanwhile, her bottom half was kicking Megan in the shins.

"Shark Boy to the rescue!" said Edwin. He scrambled up Megan's back, peeled a piece of tape from her cardboard helmet, slapped it on the doll's chin, and ripped it away.

And Princess Nurbison became a happy, smiling, broken-in-half doll again.

Edwin and Megan hugged like two koalas.

"Megan, you're my best chum in the world!" said Edwin.

"Can I be your jester again?" said Megan. "I thought up a new joke.

How do you keep cool at a football match?
You stand next to a fan!"

Everybody laughed—even Emperor
Nurbison. But he wasn't laughing in the
nice way.

"FOO HOO HOO HOO! This
is just the beginning!"

"Here we go," said Minister Jill.

Nurbison grabbed Miss Dolly-Chops
from the throne.

"She's still got plenty of hair, and my
beard will soon grow back! I shall make
new dolls! And *this* time I'll fix them so
they obey me! And with my invincible
legions of dolls I shall—"

Miss Dolly-Chops was suddenly torn
from the emperor's grasp.

"So that's where she is!" said old Empress Veronica. "What do you think you're doing, Nurbison? Stealing from your own mother! A frail, helpless old lady!"

The frail, helpless old lady put the emperor in a headlock.

"I'm—I'm sorry, Mom . . . ," whimpered Emperor Nurbison.

"Sorry's not good enough!" said the empress.

"I'm going to drag you home by the nose and spank you with a candlestick. A spiky candlestick."

She felt around his face for a few moments. There was no sign of a nose at all. He just didn't seem to have one.

"Well, an ear will do," said Veronica.

"OW! OW. OWW!"

said the emperor as his mom hauled him away.

What We've All Learned

After every adventure, King Edwin and his friends would gather on the village green to talk about what they'd learned. So when all the Nurbison dolls had been cleared away, that's just what they did.

First, one of the peasants stood up.

"We peasants have learned something," she said. "We've learned not to buy toys from evil emperors. From now on, we will get them only from recognized toy outlets with good safety standards."

Minister Jill
stood up.

"I've learned
something," said
Minister Jill. "I've
learned that to
get the job done,
sometimes we
need to work with
people we don't
always like. Also,
I learned that
King Edwin is
the cleverest and
bravest king there
is. But I sort of
knew that already."

Centurion Alisha stood up.

"I've learned that we palace guards need to be better at defending this kingdom," said Alisha. "We've let it get invaded a couple of times now. That's embarrassing. Look at me. This is my embarrassed face."

Everybody looked at Alisha. Her embarrassed face looked just the same as her angry face, or her happy face.

Baxter the Hermit would have stood up at about this time, but he was still in the kitchen, upside down in a pot, pretending to be a plant.

Then King Edwin and Megan the Jester stood up together.

"We've learned something really big!" said Megan. "We've learned that even the best of friends can sometimes make each other sad."

"But if they make up," said Edwin, "they can be best friends all over again!"

"And what's more . . . ," said Megan.

Everyone waited for her to finish.

But she couldn't think of anything extra to say. So she did a dance. Then she fell over. The people laughed and cheered.

"Now let's *all* play superheroes!" said Megan.

FOOTSIE

PROFESSOR STRIPER

ULTIMATE MINISTER

HARE KID

DEERSK8R

EQUUS

NORSE FELLER

SHARK BOY

THE HUMAN MAN

THAT MONKEY

GYMNASTICA

SUPERSHINYHEAD

POWER HAMSTER

That night, as Globulus went to bed in his tiny room in the emperor's castle, clutching a mug of cold spider's milk, he heard a sharp knock.

"Kind of, like, I suppose, um, sort of, I guess, I reckon, sort of, um, yeah, like, you know, er, so, kind of, like, I suppose, um, er, well, kind of, like, so, er, well, you know, come in," said Globulus, but Emperor Nurbison had already flung the door open.

"Globulus!" said the emperor. "I really don't know why I did this, but I made you a doll of my handsome self."

He delved into his flapping cloak and pulled out a little Nurbison doll.

"It isn't magic. Mother has all the magic hair now. But here it is anyway. And with it, this."

Nurbison placed a little Globulus doll next to it.

"Wow, like, a matching set!" said Globulus. "You and me! That's like, kind of amazing, and sort of just what I wanted, and thank you."

"Now sleep," said the emperor. "You have to get up and work for me again in half an hour."

The emperor left Globulus, then prowled through the dark passages of his castle, back to his own room.

Then he stopped. And thought.

I just gave Globulus a present. I did something nice for someone. How did that happen? That's not me. I never do anything nice for anybody. I am the evil emperor!

Then he realized: All those weeks of pretending to be nice had changed him, ever so slightly. There was now a tiny, teensy-weensy bit of good in him.

"Well, you mutant part of me that is good, I shall defeat you!" spat Nurbison. "Yes, I shall! By becoming even more evil than ever before! SQUEE HEE H— Ahem, I mean,

FOO HOO HOO HOO!"

In Edwinland, King Edwin was going to bed, too. Playing superheroes had made him super tired. Minister Jill tucked him in.

"I've had a lot of surprises on our adventures, Jill," said the young king. "But none as big as the first time I saw a *living doll.*"

"You sleep now, Edwin," said Jill.

"Toys that come to life!" said Edwin,
yawning. "Can you imagine a bigger
surprise than that? I can't. And I've got a
big imagination. Any time my imagination
doesn't feel big enough, I just imagine it's
a bit bigger, and then, ta-da! It really is."

"Night night," said Jill.

"But, Jill, you never said if you could
imagine a bigger— "

But she was already gone.

In the hallway, Minister Jill looked through a window to the moonlit ocean far away. She *could* think of something that would surprise Edwin even more than dolls that come to life. But she had never told anyone about it.

The End

Ask Globulus
YOUR PROBLEMS, SOLVED!

Q. *Dear Globulus,*

I have to wear glasses, but every pair of glasses I buy breaks when I hit it twelve times with a massive hammer. What can I do?

A. Hi, um, maybe you could try, you know, not hitting them twelve times with a massive hammer. Cut down to three or four times, yeah? And if you've still got the problem then maybe . . . you know . . . try not hitting them with the hammer. Like, ever. Sounds crazy, I know, but give it a go, sort of thing.

Q. *Dear Globulus,*

I grow lettuce in my garden, but the slugs keep eating it in the night. How can I stop them?

A. Slugs, yeah? Yeah. Thing about slugs is, they're not very good at, you know, jumping. Ever see a slug jump? No. Me neither. So I reckon, right, you should kind of like, put a line of hurdles in front of the lettuce patch, and there's, like, no way a slug is going to clear more than one of them. Hurdling slugs? Not going to happen. Or you could eat the slugs. Bit slimy, sure, but no worse than worms and, you know, we all eat worms, don't we?

Q. *Dear Globulus,*

My brother won't let me play with his football. What can I do?

A. You're sort of going, "I want the ball," yeah, and your brother, he's going, "I want the ball." But you got to think, yeah, about what the ball wants. Let the ball choose. And maybe you think balls don't have a mind and can't choose, but that's when you've got to draw a face on the ball, okay? 'Cause, you know, if you draw a face on something, then you give it a mind. That's how it works. Pretty sure, anyway. I once drew a face on my own face, yeah? And that sort of gave me an extra mind and my brain got double clever. Wait, what were we talking about?

Q. *Globulus!*

Why are you still answering letters? I need a custard cream cookie! NOW!

A. Hello, Emperor. Sorry, Emperor. Coming, Emperor.

ANDY RILEY has done lots of funny writing for film and TV, and he's even won prizes for it, like BAFTAs and an Emmy. For TV, Andy cowrote the scripts for David Walliams's *Gangsta Granny* and *The Boy in the Dress*, and *Robbie the Reindeer*. The films he's written for include *Gnomeo and Juliet* and *The Pirates! In an Adventure with Scientists!* Andy really loves cowboy hats, and he can do a brilliant "FOO HOO HOO."

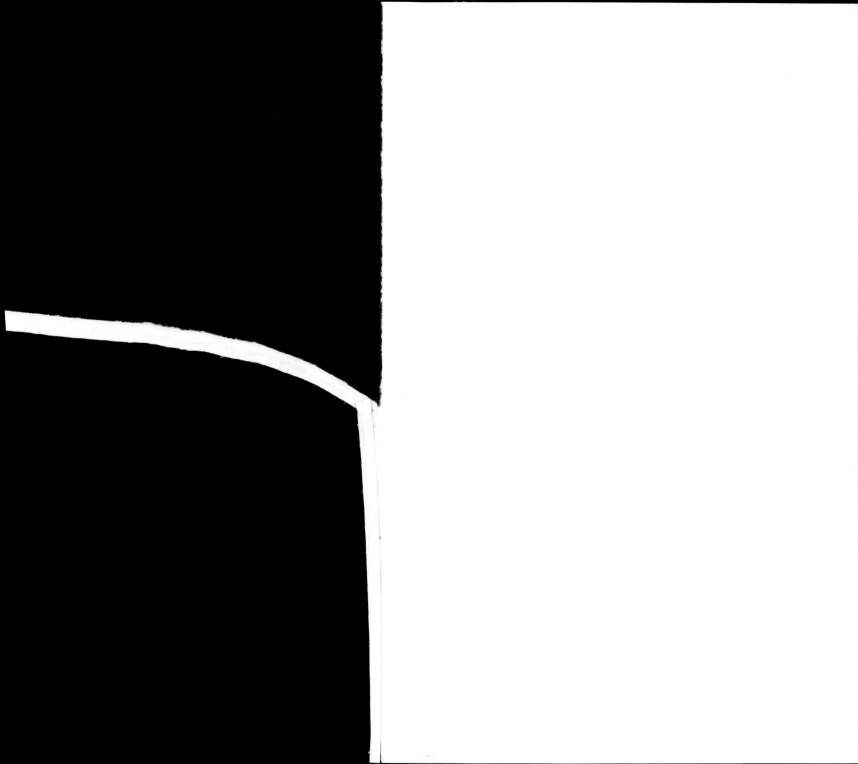